Gabriel's Ark

Sandra R. Curtis

Alef Design Group

Gabriel's Ark

LIBRARY OF CONGRESS CATALOGING-IN-PUBLICATION DATA

Curtis, Sandra R., 1950–.

    Gabriel's ark / Sandra R. Curtis.

        p.   cm.

    Summary: Because thirteen-year-old Gabe is mentally disabled and has special needs, his rabbi and family create an unconventional bar mitzvah for him, one centered around the story of Noah's ark.

    ISBN 1-881283-22-4 (alk. paper)

    [1. Bar Mitzvah—Fiction. 2. Jewish—United States—Fiction. 3. Mentally handicapped—Fiction. 4. Noah's ark—Fiction.]

    I. Title.

PZ7.C94845Gag   1998

[Fic]—dc21

                                          98-22135
                                                CIP
                                                AC

ISBN# 1-881283-22-4

ALEF DESIGN GROUP • 4423 FRUITLAND AVENUE, LOS ANGELES, CA 90058
(800) 845–0662 • (323) 582-1200 • (323) 585–0327 FAX • WWW.ALEFDESIGN.COM

MANUFACTURED IN THE UNITED STATES OF AMERICA

Dedicated to
Gabriel
and his family
for their inspiration, courage,
and friendship

Table of Contents

CHAPTER 1

The Rainbow

My brother, Gabriel, was born on a stormy winter day thirteen years ago. He still loves to hear the story of his birth, and Nana loves to tell it.

When our grandmother comes over, Gabriel tugs at her sleeve as they sit on the couch together.

"Tell about me, Nana," he says.

Nana always makes it a game. She pats the book she is reading to him.

"Oh, but this story is so wonderful," she says as she puts the book down on her lap.

"Rainbow story," Gabriel insists.

"After the book," she suggests, but Gabriel shakes his head.

"Now," he demands.

Nana always gives in.

"All right," she agrees, "if you promise we can read the book after."

Gabriel nods happily. He hugs her and she kisses him on the top of his head.

"On the day you were born, there was a terrible storm. It was dark, and cold outside. The wind whipped through the trees. The rain lashed against the windows. Lightning flashed across the sky, and thunder boomed its angry voice. Suddenly, we heard a baby's soft cry. It was the sweet voice of a new life answering the angry thunder. The rain became a soft drizzle and the sun finally broke through the clouds. Soon the room was bathed in sunlight. Your dad laid a tiny bundle in my arms."

Nana turns to Gabriel and teases him. She asks, "Who do you think it was?"

"Me," he shouts. "Me!"

"Yes," she smiles. "It was you. And do you know what happened next?"

"Window," Gabriel answers quickly. He knows his part of the story by heart. Nana smiles.

"I stood by the window, holding my very first grandchild in my arms. I felt so proud. Sunshine streamed through the glass, right on your sweet face."

Gabriel squints. Nana touches his nose and he wrinkles it up.

"You didn't like the sun in your eyes," she chuckles. "But something wonderful happened, didn't it?"

"Rainbow," Gabriel replies, nodding.

"Oh, you're so right," she says. "Through the window, we saw the most beautiful rainbow arch across the sky. And what did I say?"

"Everything fine," he smiles.

"It was very fine," Nana says, hugging Gabe. "Why?"

"Rainbow sign," Gabriel recites his part of the story.

"What a good memory you have," she laughs. "I said, 'Everything will be fine. The rainbow is a sign of welcome to our new boy.'"

I've heard that story a million times, and I know that everything was not fine.

Dr. Kogan was concerned because Gabriel was so small and his heart was very weak. She explained the problem to my parents.

"Gabriel is missing some information he needs to grow normally," she explained. "Each cell of

13

our bodies has a set of instructions to tell us how to grow. Gabriel has a set of instructions missing, so he won't grow like other children. He will need a lot of special care."

CHAPTER 2

Sisters

After my parents brought Gabriel home from the hospital, Nana began coming over for a few hours every afternoon. She stayed until dinner. That way, Mama could go shopping, or to her ballet class, or even have a quiet hour to read. And Papa could see his mother when he got home from work.

"Why don't you move in with us, Mom?" Papa asked.

"You ask me every week," Nana laughed.

"You refuse every week," her son chuckled.

"I like my independence," she said as she kissed him good-bye.

A few months after Gabe was born, Mama went back to work at her law office. Then, Nana helped Clare, the babysitter. The only time Nana didn't come was when she was sick, which was hardly ever, or if she was away on a trip. Nana traveled to faraway places where she took long hikes.

"That's the only way to get to know a land and its people," she explained.

When she came back, she told Gabriel wonderful stories about all the different places she'd been and the people she'd met. Gabe especially liked to hear about the strange animals she'd seen.

Nana was still coming every day when I was born two years later. I was lucky because there was always someone to play with me. If Mama, Nana, or Clare was taking care of Gabriel, another one would play with me. They didn't just play with Gabe. The people at the hospital gave them special games to help him get stronger because Gabe was still so small and frail. They also played games that helped him learn more.

Gabriel couldn't feed or dress himself, or even walk and talk like other two year olds. He had just learned to sit up, which most six-month-old babies can do. But there was one thing Gabe did just like any two year old. He threw tantrums— terrific tantrums. When anything was new, Gabriel threw one. It could be a new food, a new shirt, a new game, or even a new person.

Gabriel also liked to laugh and be silly, like other kids his age. Papa played with me and Gabe when he got home from teaching at the university. He tickled us and played peek-a-boo. We loved his "Animal Surprise" game the most. Papa made our toy sheep moo or our cows bark. We were supposed to make the correct animal sound, but sometimes we couldn't because we were laughing so hard.

Gabriel and I were both in nursery school at the same time but we went to different schools. I went to our neighborhood nursery for half a day. Gabriel went for the whole day to a school for kids who needed special teachers. We both did puzzles, built with blocks, made sand castles, listened to stories, and played dress up.

My class had a lot more kids in it than Gabe's did. Everyone in his class got lots of special help. They learned things like how to button their shirts and how to use the bathroom. They worked on speaking clearly and following directions. Gabe worked on walking. He didn't take his first steps until he was almost five because his muscles still weren't very strong and he couldn't balance very well. He was five before he could really walk.

When Gabe was six and I was four, our sister Rachel was born. Nana kept coming, of course, and Papa kept trying to get her to move in with us. She kept refusing.

"I like my independence," she'd say.

Having a baby sister was a big change at our house, but it wasn't the biggest change for our family.

CHAPTER 3

A New School

Gabe was going to start a new school after the summer. Blake Street School was huge. They had lots of neat things to help the kids, like special computers and ramps for children in wheelchairs, and even an indoor pool so the kids could do exercises in the water. The only problem was that the school was really far from our house. So Gabe was going to live with Marge's family during the week. Another boy from Blake lived there, too. A school bus would pick them up and drop them off from Marge's every day. Gabe would come home on weekends.

Even though I was only four, I knew that the next year I would be going to our neighborhood kindergarten. "Why can't Gabe go to Emerson school next year with me?" I asked Mama one night when she was tucking me in bed.

"He needs the kind of help the teachers at his new school can give him, Leah," she answered.

"But I can help him," I pleaded.

"You help him so much already," Mama smiled. "You look at books together, and you play with him. But you need to do your work at Emerson, and Gabe needs to do his work at Blake School."

"He won't like it," I warned. "New things make him cry."

"He'll have lots of people to help him," she assured me.

"He'll be scared," I argued.

"We're all scared when we start something new," she replied.

"But they won't understand him," I cried. "He needs us!"

"Of course he does," Mama said, hugging me tightly, "and we need him. Gabe will be fine, Leah. I've spent lots of time at Blake and with Marge. It's the best way for him to do his learning. I'm not worried about his new school, or about him living with Marge's family, but what I am worried about is how much I'll miss him. How about you?"

I started to cry. Mama stroked my hair. I knew I would miss my brother a lot, even though I did have a new baby sister.

"When will we see him, Mama?"

"Every Shabbat," she answered. "I'll pick him up on Friday afternoon and he'll spend the weekend with us. Every vacation, too."

"What about Nana? Will she keep coming every day?"

"Why don't you ask her yourself?"

Mama dialed Nana's number and gave me the phone.

"Nana, will you still come every day even when Gabe is at his new school?" I asked, holding the phone tightly to my ear.

"I wouldn't miss it for the world, sweetheart," she said.

"Goodnight, Nana," I said. "I love you."

"Laila tov, Leah," she said. "I love you, too."

CHAPTER 4

Family Stories

Nana kept coming to our house every afternoon, and she kept amusing us with her stories. One she really liked to tell was how I taught Gabriel to eat by himself. I don't remember doing it, but Nana wouldn't say it if it wasn't true.

"Leah, you and Gabe used to sit right next to each other at the table in your high chairs. He would watch you pick up food between your thumb and your first finger, like you were pinching something. Gabriel tried to do what you were doing. He dropped lots of carrots and raisins and other food, but he kept working at it and pretty soon, he could feed himself. It was such a big step because before you showed him, someone always had to feed Gabe."

Rachel must have heard that feeding story at least a hundred times by the time she was three. She decided she wanted to help Gabriel learn something, too. When he was home on the weekend, she started playing Papa's "Animal Surprise" game with him. Over the years, it grew into their special game.

"Woof, woof," Rachel would bark, showing Gabe a lion from his favorite toy, Noah's ark.

"No dog," Gabe would laugh. "Roar! Roar! Lion roars!" He'd make a fierce roar and Rachel would pretend to be very scared.

When Gabe laughed his eyes became tiny slits that made him look like his family came from Asia. We don't, though. He looked Asian even when he wasn't laughing because he was born with a small fold of skin over his eyelids like they have.

In the afternoons, Rachel watched *Sesame Street* with Gabe. He really liked Bert and Ernie.

Rachel learned to talk like Ernie to make Gabriel laugh. But when she talked like Count Dracula, he cried.

"Count scary," he fussed.

Rachel and Gabe practiced the alphabet together. She put up magnet letters on the refrigerator.

"A, B, C," they recited together.

Sometimes, Rachel mixed the letters up by accident and Gabriel would laugh. Later, Rachel mixed them up on purpose.

"Here's the letter O," Rachel would say, but she'd point to the P.

"P," Gabriel would shout. "P! P! P! Not O."

"Oh, I goofed," Rachel would laugh. "I can't trick you, can I, Gabey?"

"P, P, P!" Gabe would say, poking at the letter.

"How do you know it's a P?" Rachel would ask.

Gabe would turn around and wiggle his bottom at her. "P has a tail," he'd answer.

They'd both fall on the floor laughing.

That's how Rachel found her special way to help Gabriel. Now Nana has a story to tell about how Rachel helped Gabe learn the alphabet.

CHAPTER 5

Homecoming

Gabriel came home every Friday afternoon. He stayed with us all weekend and on Sunday night, Mama or Papa drove him back to Marge's. Gabe called her house his "school house."

Six years went by and Rachel and I grew. Like most sisters, we played together a lot and sometimes we argued. If I felt sad about not having Gabriel living with us, I talked with Mama, or Papa, or Nana. They felt sad sometimes, too, but they knew it was the best place for Gabriel. Nana said it was like when Papa went off to college. She missed him, but she knew he was learning the things he needed.

Rachel didn't understand how I felt because she didn't remember what it was like to have Gabriel living at home. He went to live at Marge's when she was a baby.

Other things were changing, too. Nana was getting older. She didn't go on so many trips. She got sick a little more, and she didn't say she liked her independence so much when Papa asked her to move in.

"Someday soon, I think she'll say yes," Papa told me one night.

The whole family looked forward to Fridays. Not only did Gabriel come home, but it was the end of the work week, the school week, and it was also Shabbat, the Jewish Sabbath. Shabbat was our special day of rest, the same as when God rested from creating the world. Mama made a special dinner every Friday night with flowers, candles, wine and freshly baked hallah. Rachel and I helped Nana knead and braid the egg bread when we came home from school. We brushed the top with egg to make it shiny. While it was baking, we helped Nana set the table. We cut flowers from outside and arranged them for the table. Before we knew it, the house smelled sweet and delicious.

Just about that time, Mama honked the horn as she pulled into the driveway with Gabriel. Rachel and I ran outside to greet them. Rachel raced me to the car to open the door first.

"I win!" she shouted.

I let her win. What's the big deal about opening a car door anyway?

Gabriel was always excited when they drove up. His hands moved around like he was fanning himself.

"Leah! Rachel!" he shouted, waving from the window as Mama pulled into the driveway.

Gabriel's voice always sounded like he had a cold.

"Guess who's hiding in the ark?" Rachel asked Gabe.

"Tiger?" Gabe asked. He squinted his eyes and tilted his head to the side. That was his way of showing he was really curious.

"Let's see," I said, helping him out of the car. Even though Gabe was two years older than me, I was taller and stronger than him. I felt like I was his big sister, instead of him being my big brother. I helped him up the stairs to our front door because he was still not very steady when he walked.

At the door of his room, Gabriel let go of my hand and rushed toward the wooden ark on the floor by his bed. He leaned forward so much when he walked, he looked like he was going to fall over any minute. Rachel raced in front of him.

"Not yet! " she called. "You have to guess first!"

Rachel clasped both hands together and swung her arms from side to side. She lumbered around the room, pretending to be an elephant. "Squeak, squeak," she joked.

"No mouse, silly," he laughed.

"Elephant!"

"E-phe-lants!" giggled Rachel. Mixing up the sounds in a word was a new way they played "Animal Surprise."

"E-le-phants!" said Gabriel firmly, pulling out two plastic gray elephants with long white tusks. He clutched them happily to his chest.

Even after all these years, the ark and its animals are still Gabriel's favorite toy.

CHAPTER 6

Shabbat Dinner

On Friday nights after Papa got home from work, everyone washed up for dinner. Nana helped Gabe get ready. Papa looked forward to his candlelight dinner at the end of each week.

"Shabbat reminds me of how lucky I am," he'd say. "It's my special time with everyone I love best in the world."

A quiet calm came over our house as Mama and Nana lit the Shabbat candles. Rachel and I loved to watch them close their eyes and circle the flames with their hands, pulling the warmth and light into them.

Papa would close his eyes as he sang the kiddush over the wine. Gabriel watched the shadows from the candles dance on the wall. He moved his body slowly, swaying like the flames. We joined Papa in the blessing, but sometimes we rushed. Papa would make sure to sing a little slower if we got going too fast. We couldn't wait to bless the hallah so we could tear into the steaming loaf for a piece of its soft middle. After we said the blessing over the bread, we went around the table wishing everyone, "Shabbat Shalom," a good Sabbath, and sang songs.

We had a funny hallah song we sang each week for Gabe. It was to the tune of "I Have a Little Dreidel" and it goes like this:

> I made a little hallah.
> I made it all myself.
> I put it in the oven.
> I put in on the shelf.
>
> Now, "Listen little hallah.
> You must not run away.
> I need you for the Shabbat.
> Oh, hallah, please do stay."

I didn't mean to touch it
But, oh, it smelled so nice.
I took a little nibble.
I took a little bite.

Then before I knew it
The pantry shelf was bare.
There wasn't any hallah.
The hallah wasn't there.

"Who ate the hallah, Gabe?" Rachel always asked.

"I did!" he'd giggle, nibbling the tasty bread.

Once we finished the blessings and singing, we sat down for dinner. This particular Shabbat, Mama had something special to tell us.

"Kids," she began, "it's Gabriel's thirteenth birthday in a few months. Papa and I spoke to Rabbi Cohen about doing a special bar mitzvah. He's coming over on Sunday to discuss it.

"In Jewish tradition, young people learn to read from the Torah, around the time they turn thirteen. The ceremony is called a bar or bat mitzvah. It's not that they're really grown up all of a sudden, but they're on the road to becoming adults. Kids spend a long time learning to read Hebrew and to chant a weekly portion. They read from a Torah scroll that was written by hand on animal skins. Just looking at it makes me feel like a part of history because Jews from all over the world have been reading and studying the same Torah for more than two thousand years. Afterwards, kids feel really proud and their families are really proud, too, because they've joined all the generations before them in becoming a b'nai mitzvah."

The ceremony isn't like a birthday. On your birthday you're the center of attention, but you don't have to do anything. You just had to be born. At a bar or bat mitzvah, you're the center of attention because you read from the Torah.

Then you explain the meaning of the portion to the whole congregation. It's a really big job. I can't wait for mine in a couple of years.

Gabriel, however, didn't know any of this. He wasn't excited. A bar mitzvah was something new, and when something was new, Gabriel threw a tantrum. This time, he threw his fork on the floor and started to cry.

"No rabbi! No rabbi!"

"Gabe," Papa said gently, but in a firm voice, "pick up your fork."

Gabe picked up the fork, but he continued shouting, "No rabbi! No mitzvah!"

"You like Rabbi Cohen," Papa reminded him. "He tells stories like Noah's ark, remember? And we'll all be here with you, even Nana."

CHAPTER 7

Rabbi Cohen's Visit

On Sunday when Rabbi Cohen arrived for brunch, I was practicing the piano. Gabriel was playing on the living room floor with his ark and animals. Rachel was drawing a rainbow on construction paper, carefully outlining a billowy white cloud at each end.

"That's beautiful," admired Rabbi Cohen.

Rachel looked up from her drawing table.

"A rainbow came out when Gabe was born," she explained.

"What a very special welcome," smiled the Rabbi.

We ate bagels and lox and eggs for brunch.

When Rabbi Cohen finished his coffee, he asked Gabriel to show him his ark.

"Is someone hiding in there?" the Rabbi asked Gabe.

"Guess," Gabriel answered. He swung his arms together in front of his nose. "Squeak, squeak," he joked.

"Watch out," Rachel warned Rabbi Cohen. "He likes to trick you."

"Thanks for the tip," the Rabbi whispered to Rachel. "Is it a mouse or a...?" He stopped to wonder, scratching his head.

"Look," Gabriel urged.

The rabbi opened the ark and took out the toy.

"Elephant!" clapped Gabe.

"It looks like a hepphalump to me," smiled Rabbi Cohen.

"Now that I've seen what's hiding in your ark, you must come to the synagogue and see what's hiding in mine. Bring your animals and I'll tell you the story of Noah's ark. We'll sing songs, too."

"No songs!" cried Gabe, flapping his hands wildly.

I caught his hands in mine.

"New things are hard for him," I explained. I felt embarrassed by Gabe's tantrum. I wished he would behave. "We're all going to come with you, Mama, Papa, Nana, me and Rachel."

"And you can all learn something for the service," added Rabbi Cohen, "just like Gabe."

CHAPTER 8

The Synagogue Visit

A couple of weeks later, we visited the synagogue. Two men were kneeling outside the main entrance setting bricks in wet cement for a new wheelchair ramp.

"Look, Gabe!" Rachel exclaimed. "It's just like the ramp your animals march up to get into your ark! Let's pretend we're horses prancing up."

She pulled Gabe along the newly laid brick path, lifting her knees high in the air.

"Hey…get off the wet bricks, you two!" yelled one of the workmen.

Rachel pulled Gabe off as fast as she could and down to the waiting room outside Rabbi Cohen's

office. Gabriel couldn't sit still. He darted back and forth between us. When the Rabbi opened his door, Gabe slid behind Mama.

"Hi, everyone. It's good to see you." He leaned down to speak to my brother. "So, Gabe, did you bring your ark?" Rabbi Cohen asked.

Gabriel pointed down at the bag in Mama's hand.

"Good. Let's take it upstairs."

We followed Rabbi Cohen into the empty sanctuary. He took Gabriel's hand and helped him climb the stairs onto the bimah. The Torah was kept behind the wooden doors of the aron ha-kodesh, the holy ark.

"What do you think is hiding in my ark?" the Rabbi asked, leading him up to the wooden doors.

"Elephant?" Gabriel guessed, squinting his eyes and tilting his head.

Rabbi Cohen peeked inside the doors.

"No hepphalumps in here, but there's something else that's very special. Let's see." Gabriel helped the rabbi open the ark to reveal three Torah scrolls, adorned in breast plates, velvet covers and silver crowns.

"These scrolls contain the laws and stories of the Jewish people, Gabe. Your Noah story is in here. It's hiding in a special language. Come see."

Rabbi Cohen unrolled the Torah scroll to the Noah portion. "You hold the pointer and I'll read," he said, helping Gabe place the yad at the beginning of the story.

Rabbi Cohen began chanting in Hebrew but switched to English to hold Gabriel's attention.

"So Noah collected the animals two by two and led them up the ramp into the ark."

"Two by two," Gabriel repeated.

He set up his animals on the bimah stairs, then paraded them by pairs into his ark at the top while the Rabbi continued reading the story.

"It rained for forty days and forty nights. Water covered the entire earth. When the rain finally stopped and the water went down, God set a rainbow in the sky as a promise never to destroy life on earth again."

"We need a really big rainbow over the ark," Rachel decided, "so we can all remember that promise."

"If you draw one, I'll put it up," the rabbi promised. He knelt beside Gabriel. "I want you to learn to say the Shema with your sisters for your bar mitzvah."

"No Shema!" Gabe cried, shaking his head and pounding two animals together.

"We'll do it in English," I said, hoping to calm him down.

Gabriel shook his head. "No. No Shema!"

Rabbi Cohen shook his finger at a toy elephant, pretending to scold it. "What are you doing out of line, you silly hepphalump! Into the ark!"

Gabriel relaxed. He shook his finger at the animal, too. "Into the ark, silly e-le-phant."

Rabbi Cohen smiled and spoke softly. "When we recite the Shema, Gabriel, we're declaring that we are one people, the people Israel, and we have one God."

Gabriel continued marching his animals two-by-two into the ark.

"You are part of that people, Gabe," said the Rabbi, "just like every person in your family. We must each learn as much as we can and do the best we can to help make a better world. That's why we study the stories in the Torah."

After the Rabbi returned the Torah to the ark, Papa, Rachel and I followed him outside. Mama and Nana helped Gabe collect his animals.

"Such a rabbi," Nana whispered to Mama.

"He's so wonderful with Gabe and this is an extraordinary synagogue. When I was a girl, children like Gabriel weren't welcome in shul."

They joined us outside as the Rabbi was asking me a question.

"Can you read what it says above the doors, Leah?" he asked.

"For My house shall be called a house of prayer for all peoples," I read aloud.

"Isaiah, the prophet, said that. We want everyone to feel welcome here. Each of us is special in our own way, because we are all created in God's image. We should feel as safe in here as the animals did in the ark."

Gabriel tugged at Papa's sleeve. "Go home."

Rabbi Cohen laughed. "I guess we're finished today. Gabe, we're all going to help make your bar mitzvah very special. That's a promise, just like God and the rainbow."

CHAPTER 9

Studying

During the following weeks, Hebrew melodies floated through our house like the wonderful smell of Nana's chicken soup. Rabbi Cohen was helping each of us learn a part for the service.

In most homes where a bar or bat mitzvah was coming up, the boy or girl would be practicing their Torah portion. But in our house Mama and Papa were practicing. Gabriel had taken on what he could do for his bar mitzvah, so they decided to chant his Noah portion.

Nana was reading Gabe's haftarah portion. The haftarah for Noah came from the Book of Isaiah. He's the prophet who said, "My house shall be a house of prayer for all people." In the

Noah haftarah, Isaiah reminds the Jewish people of God's promise never to flood the earth again and of God's loyalty to them.

Rachel and I were going to recite the Shema in Hebrew and English with Gabriel. When Gabe was home on Fridays, we tried get him to practice the prayer with us. No matter what we tried, he always refused. Sometimes he even refused to talk to Rabbi Cohen when he came to see how we were doing. He stayed in his room, playing with his ark and animals.

The rabbi listened to each of us do our parts.

"It's so nice of you to do a house visit," Nana said him after her practice.

"I've never had a whole family working on a bar mitzvah together before," the Rabbi replied. "It's a real treat for me."

Before he left, Rabbi Cohen always went in to see Gabe. I don't know if they practiced or just talked about the animals.

A week before Gabriel's bar mitzvah, Rachel and I tried to practice with Gabe while we were setting the dinner table. He refused.

"It's only a week until your bar mitzvah, Gabe," I said feeling very irritated.

"No Shema!" he cried.

"You have to practice the part you're going to say with us in synagogue," I argued.

"No synagogue!" he protested.

"Not synagogue," Rachel joked. "Silly dog!"

"Rachel!" I yelled.

I didn't think this was the time to add a new word like ephelants and hepphalumps, to "Animal Surprise," but Rachel thought it might help.

"It's his bar mitzvah and he won't even practice!" I charged around the kitchen complaining. "He's twelve going on two, not thirteen!"

"Be patient, Leah," Mama added. "Gabe will do his part in his own time and in his own way."

"Well, he doesn't have much time left!" I snapped. "What if he won't say the prayer at the service? He could refuse, you know! It'll be so embarrassing. People won't understand."

"I know how you feel, but if he refuses, you and Rachel go on without him. If standing in front of the ark is the most your brother can do, it will be enough. Everyone will understand. We each have to do the best we can, remember?"

"Rainbows are what I do best," said Rachel. "Can I use a white sheet to draw one for over the ark?"

"I'll get you one after dinner," Mama offered.

When the dishes were done, Rachel began coloring a huge rainbow while I did my homework. Nana heard Gabe playing in his room. He was repeating the Shema to his animals.

"Don't worry," she told me later. "Gabe will do his part."

"I hope so," I said, getting up from the table to see how Rachel's rainbow was coming along.

She was drawing the outline of clouds at each end.

"Look, Nana," I noticed, "the clouds look like hands reaching out to everyone."

"How lovely," Nana smiled.

CHAPTER 10
The Big Day

The next Saturday, our house bustled with excitement from early in the morning. It was a brisk, autumn day. The sun shone brightly in the crisp air. A new batch of leaves was scattered over the lawn and sidewalk, like confetti on New Year's Eve. Everyone was dressed in their Shabbat best for Gabriel's bar mitzvah, everyone that is, except Gabriel.

"No rabbi!" he protested.

"He's gonna ruin it," I muttered, as Mama brushed my hair.

"Oh, don't be such a grump," she warned. "Leave it to Papa. Gabe will be fine."

I heard Papa coaxing Gabriel.

"Better pack your animals in the bag," he said. "They want to visit Rabbi Cohen's ark today because it's your special day and the Rabbi is going to tell their special story."

His coaxing worked. Gabriel put his toys in the backpack. Once they were safely in the bag, Gabriel let Papa help him dress.

Finally, the whole family was ready. A special surprise greeted us at the synagogue.

Balloons arched over the entrance above the new ramp. They were arranged in the colors of a rainbow.

"Balloons! Balloons!" Gabriel shouted, clapping his hands.

"It's our sign of welcome to everyone," Papa said, as we walked towards the ramp.

Gabriel tugged at Rachel's dress. "Be a horse," he urged.

"Not today," I said. "It's not time to play."

"Let's walk up the ramp two by two," Rachel suggested.

"Like the animals," said Gabe.

"You go first," Rachel told him. "Pick a partner."

Gabriel linked arms with Nana and they marched into the sanctuary together. I went up the ramp with Rachel, then came Mama and Papa, followed by the Rabbi and the Cantor. Soon, everyone followed suit, walking in two by two. Dr. Kogan even came with her husband. Rabbi Cohen welcomed them to shul.

Dr. Kogan noticed Rachel's rainbow arching over the aron ha-kodesh. "Who did that beautiful rainbow?" she asked.

"The family artist," Rabbi Cohen replied, pointing to Rachel.

Before he went onto the bimah to begin the service, the Rabbi stopped before us in the front row to give our family a special greeting.

"Shabbat Shalom," the Rabbi said, shaking Papa's hand. "This will be a wonderful service."

"We're looking forward to it," Papa smiled.

Rabbi Cohen leaned down and whispered to Rachel, "Your rainbow's a big hit." She beamed proudly. Then he crouched down in front of Gabriel. "Are your hepphalumps ready?" Gabe looked away, hiding his face in Papa's sleeve. "Do the best you can, Gabe, and everything will be fine."

I sure hoped so.

CHAPTER 11

The Service

The service began. Gabe played with his animals on the seat between me and Rachel. When he got restless, Papa took him outside for a while.

"It's almost time to say your prayer," Papa said.

Gabe's eyes filled with tears. His lower lip trembled and his hands moved nervously as he and Papa sat beside Mama.

"Remember Rabbi Cohen's promise," said Mama gently. "We're all here to help."

I held my hand out to Gabe. Rachel picked up his ark filled with animals. Clutching my hand and Rachel's arm, Gabriel walked onto the bimah between us. Rachel set Gabe's toy ark at the base of the synagogue's ark. Then, together, we opened the doors of the aron ha-kodesh.

Rachel and I began to sing. "Shema Yisrael…"

The congregation joined in the blessing, but Gabriel remained silent. I tugged his hand.

"Come on, Gabe."

"No!"

He sat down, right on the bimah in front of the entire congregation and dumped his animals out of the ark! My face burned with embarrassment.

Rachel and I continued alone.

"Hear, O Israel…"

As soon as we finished, I rushed off the bimah as fast as I could and buried my head in Mama's shoulder. I felt Rachel sink into her seat beside me.

I heard Rabbi Cohen tell Gabe, "Let's read Noah's story."

"Wait," Gabe whispered to him.

Silence blanketed the synagogue. Rachel nudged me. I looked up. Gabriel was picking up his toy ark. He opened its doors and turned it to the open ark before him. Slowly, he raised his ark towards the aron ha-kodesh. His high, nasal voice pierced the stillness.

"Hear, Israel," he said. "One God. Rainbow promise."

Rabbi Cohen smiled at Gabriel as he lifted the Torah. The congregation rose, joining in a chorus that filled the sanctuary like a fresh breeze after a storm. I couldn't believe it. Gabriel said the prayer his way, all by himself on the bimah. He even added the part about the rainbow. I hugged Rachel and Mama. I felt like cheering and clapping, but you don't do that in synagogue. So I sang the loudest and proudest of all.

Standing on the bimah under the rainbow, Rabbi Cohen handed the Torah to Nana, who passed it to Mama and Papa. They helped Gabriel hold it in the tradition of passing the Torah from one generation to the next.

Papa held one Torah and the Cantor gave Mama another one to carry.

"Come on, girls," the Rabbi beckoned us.

We marched along the aisles leading the Torah procession as the congregation sang.

Rachel and I each held one of Gabriel's arms. He was beaming. I have never seen him so happy around so many people.

Of course, I would have liked him to say the Shema in Hebrew with us, but it didn't really matter. God hears prayers in every language. Gabe did the best that he could. In fact, he did better than anyone expected, except Nana. She knew he'd do fine. Maybe Rabbi Cohen did, too.

Rachel and I kept Gabriel busy while Mama and Papa chanted the Torah portion and then Nana sang the haftarah.

When the service was over, Nana beamed, "You see," she hugged me, "everything turned out fine. The rainbow is a sign of welcome to our young man."